The Gold Dust Letters

Other Avon Camelot Books by
Janet Taylor Lisle

LOOKING FOR JULIETTE

JANET TAYLOR LISLE is the author of seven books for children—*The Gold Dust Letters*, the first in a four-book series starring the Investigators of the Unknown; *Forest* and *The Lampfish of Twill*, both *School Library Journal* Best Books of the Year; *The Dancing Cats of Applesap*; *Sirens and Spies*, an ALA Notable Book; *The Great Dimpole Oak*; and *Afternoon of the Elves*, a 1990 Newbery Honor Book.

She and her family live on the seacoast of Rhode Island.

The Gold Dust Letters

JANET TAYLOR LISLE

AVON BOOKS
A division of
The Hearst Corporation
1350 Avenue of the Americas
New York, New York 10019

Published by arrangement with Orchard Books, New York
Library of Congress Catalog Card Number: 93-11806
ISBN: 0-380-72516-9
RL: 4.9

First Avon Camelot Printing: May 1996

Printed in the U.S.A.

OPM 10 9 8 7 6 5 4 3

The Gold Dust Letters

Chapter One

Angela Harrall took an interest in magic. Not the silly hocus-pocus of birthday party magicians, or the dumb card tricks her older brother was always playing on her. Angela wasn't a stupid person. But the real magic that is present at unexplainable happenings, the power that haunts a house or works quietly behind the scenes in secret, hidden worlds—oh yes, Angela adored that sort of thing. She was a believer in the unknown, and that was why she wrote her crazy letter in the first place.

Georgina Rusk wouldn't have done it. She believed in the unknown, too, more or less, but not in writing to it. And little Poco Lambert, well . . . she was an animal-lover who spoke mostly to pets.

"I can't believe you actually wrote to her," Georgina said irritably, on the Saturday morning that Angela's mysterious answer appeared. "I mean it's so ridiculous, writing a letter to your fairy godmother. Nobody bothers with that stuff anymore."

The three friends were at the Rusks' house, lounging on their big back lawn. The day was a warm one, one of those early October beauties when summer takes a last wistful turn before giving up the stage to autumn's chill.

"Well, I bothered with it, and I got an answer back," Angela replied. "It was on the mantelpiece in the living room when I came downstairs for breakfast this morning."

"So? Anybody could have written a letter and put it there. In case you've forgotten, three other people live in your house: your mother, your brother, and your father."

"And your Siamese cat," Poco said sweetly to Angela. "Don't forget her."

"Her cat!" exclaimed Georgina. "Good grief!"

"Siamese cats are very talented," Poco went on. "People don't yet know all the things they can do."

Georgina rolled her eyes. "All right, where is this fantastic letter?" she asked Angela. "You said you were going to show us, and you didn't even bring it with you."

"Yes I did."

"Well, where is it? I suppose you're going to tell us it's invisible. It's from one of those fairy godmothers that only appear to people who believe in them. Like Tinkerbell. But if we clap our hands together really hard and fast, the magic will go to work and—"

"George, ssh!" said Poco. "Look!"

While Georgina was talking, Angela had reached into the cotton vest she was wearing and taken something out of an inside pocket. It was a piece of paper, rolled up, with a thin gold thread tied around the middle. She held the paper up triumphantly for them to see, and when she did, a very fine golden dust flew out of one end and fell to the grass in a shimmering stream.

"Wow!" exclaimed Poco, reaching out to the place in the grass where the dust had fallen. She tried to pick some up, but it had disappeared.

Georgina said nothing, but her eyes widened.

"That happens every time I go to open the letter!" Angela exclaimed. "I can never see where it comes from. Look, there's nothing inside."

She unrolled the paper, which was thin but stiffer than ordinary paper. It made a crinkly sound as it came unfurled. Angela showed Poco and Georgina the open letter. There wasn't a bit of gold dust on it anywhere. Strange-looking purple writing covered the page. The friends leaned forward together and read the following:

With great honor I present myself: Pilaria of the Kingdom of the Faeries, Eighth Tribe, Fourth Earth, Under the Sun-Star Aravan, May It Shine on Our Land Forever and Ever.

ANGELA HARRALL:

Your message has been received. Unfortunately, boxes of chocolates like the one you requested have long been out of stock. A hundred years ago they were all the rage, but fashions change. The kingdom has not filled such an order in fifty or sixty years and no longer prepares them. We are sorry that we cannot grant your wish in this matter.

Respectfully,
The Gray-Eyed Faerie,
PILARIA

"Good grief, Angela. What kind of chocolates did you ask for?" Georgina demanded, after she had read all the way through.

Angela blushed. She was a stocky child who was known for her excellent appetite. "Well . . . I read about a box of candy that could never be finished," she explained. "The girl in the story asked for one from her fairy godmother, and she got it. It was great. Whenever she put the cover back on, all the chocolates she'd eaten grew back again so she could start all over."

There was a long silence while everyone read the letter again. And again. The purple script was beautiful. It descended the page in marvelous loops and swirls and looked vaguely Chinese. Pilaria's signature was elegant beyond words.

"This was not done by a Siamese cat," Poco announced finally.

"No." Georgina tested the paper's thinness between two fingers. "It might be old airmail paper," she said doubtfully.

"It's too stiff," Angela said.

"I've never seen writing like this," Georgina said. "Or ink this color." She paused. "But the letter is stupid. Nobody would ever believe such baloney. 'Eighth Tribe, Fourth Earth, Under the Sun-Star Aravan.' I mean really!"

Angela looked at her angrily. She rolled the letter back up fast—it seemed to want to roll up by itself anyway—and slipped the circle of gold thread around it. She was preparing to put it back in her vest pocket when Georgina gasped. Poco sat forward, her eyes round with astonishment. "The gold dust!" she cried. "There it is again!"

A rather larger amount of dust had dropped out of the letter and was falling in a shining river toward the ground. But once there, the stuff completely disappeared, just as it had the first time.

Angela shook her head helplessly. "That's what always happens," she said, tucking the amazing letter back into her inside pocket. "The gold dust never runs out. There's always more inside no matter how much you look and look and can't see how there could be."

Chapter Two

There was no way, after seeing Angela's letter, that the friends could continue sitting in a backyard, however beautiful the day. Georgina demanded to be taken at once to the mantelpiece where the letter had been discovered. She wanted to know when the letter was found, who was in the house at the time, where they were—having breakfast? still in bed?—what had happened the night before, and a hundred other details.

Angela was very pleased by this flurry of questions, which showed that Georgina might not be so disbelieving as she pretended. She agreed to allow Georgina to inspect the mantelpiece on the condition that she tell no one about the Gray-Eyed Faerie's letter. It was to be a secret until they found out more.

At this point, Poco announced that she would go to Angela's house, too, but not to see the mantelpiece. Having spoken with such authority about the mysterious talents of Siamese cats, she wanted to look more closely at Angela's. Perhaps, after all, she'd underestimated it.

"Do you know that Siamese cats were the royal cats of kings and queens?" she asked the friends as they walked, rather fast because of Georgina's impatience, along the sidewalk toward Angela's house. "They lived in temples and palaces in the country of Siam, and got used to lying around on silk pillows and peacock feathers. That's why they always look so snobby."

"*Do* they look snobby?" Georgina inquired. "Angela's always looks sound asleep to me."

"Oh, yes," Poco said. "Very beautiful but very snobby. But quite nice underneath when you get to know them. You should always give a person a chance and not judge by what you see on the surface."

Georgina caught Angela's eye, but neither spoke. It was so like Poco to confuse animals and people. There was no use going into the matter. To Poco, animals were people, and that was that. She could see no separation.

"Well, you check out the cat while we investigate the mantel," Georgina said, rather nicely for her. "I think it's important for us not to rule out anything. And we can take a closer look at the letter when we get to Angela's room. I'd like to try to collect some of this gold dust and see what it's made of."

"You can't," Angela said. "I mean, it's uncollectible. You can't keep the dust in your hand. It just slips away. I tried it."

"Well, now *I* would like to try it," Georgina replied, in such a proud, nasty tone—as if Angela's try could not be trusted while hers was of first importance—that Angela reached protectively for the letter inside her vest.

"You can't," she said. "I'm the only one who can touch this letter."

"Angela!" Georgina came to a halt. "Don't be stupid!"

"I'm not stupid," Angela said, and the dark red flush that always showed when she was angry began to color her face. "I'm the owner of this letter. What I say is what we do."

"Angela!"

Angela had started walking again. "What I

say is what we do!" she yelled back over her shoulder to Georgina. "Or nobody is even coming into my house!"

"Okay, okay." Georgina ran to catch up. "I'm sorry, really. I didn't know you felt that way about it. Don't get so mad. I would never touch the letter if you didn't want me to. But you've got to let me come and look at that mantelpiece."

"Well, all right," said Angela, walking steadily along. "Sometimes you get so bossy."

"I'm sorry!"

During all this, Poco had kept walking. She was a good distance ahead by now, moving dreamily along the sidewalk on her elf-tiny feet. There *was* something rather otherworldly about Poco. She often acted like a person on another wavelength. She could look right at you and not hear a word you were saying. But then, out of the blue, she'd make some amazing remark that showed she was a hundred miles ahead of where you thought.

This is exactly what Poco did now.

"Wait! Wait for us!" Georgina yelled to her, but the little figure in front chugged ahead, oblivious to all. The friends had to run like Olympic racers to catch up. And when they did, and were puffing and panting by her side, Poco looked over at them with the sweetest expression and said, "I don't know why you're bothering with that mantelpiece. There won't be any clues there. What you should look for is the ink."

"The ink?" exclaimed Angela and Georgina together in astonishment.

"Yes," said Poco. "If someone in Angela's family wrote the letter, they probably wrote it there in the house. That means the bottle of purple ink would be around somewhere—say, in her mother's desk or her brother's room. If you found it, you'd know the letter was a fake. But if you didn't . . ."

"That's right!" breathed Georgina. "That's exactly right." She gazed at Poco suspiciously. "How did you figure this out? You were thinking about cats the last we knew."

Poco shrugged and looked away. A second later she had caught sight of a pair of squirrels up a tree and had stopped and begun a conversation with them. This was so embarrassing to Angela and Georgina, who did not like to be seen doing crazy things in public places, that they slunk on by her and made for Angela's house.

"Well, you two bushy-tails certainly look happy with yourselves," they heard Poco's voice say cheerfully, before they could get out of earshot. "What's going on up there in the squirrel world? What did you say? Come on down where I can hear you better."

"Good grief!" moaned Georgina. "Do you think she'll ever get over it?"

When Poco finished talking to the squirrels in the tree, she went to Angela's house and started up a conversation with Angela's Siamese, whose name was Juliette. And they had gone quite a distance—as far as tuna fish, in fact, which Juliette was very fond of, while Poco had to admit she couldn't stand even the smell—when Georgina and Angela came to join them in the living room. The two girls had searched the whole house and turned up nothing.

"Not only no purple ink, but no ink, period," Georgina said, walking over to the mantelpiece and staring at it disgustedly. Poco had been right. There were no clues there.

"And no purple pens and no purple paints!" Angela said excitedly. "No strange, stiff paper or thin gold thread, either!"

"And no gold dust, naturally." Georgina turned around to face them. "We went through every drawer and every cupboard and every closet. Mrs. Harrall wanted to know what we were looking for, so I told her I'd lost my ring." Having said this, she glanced suddenly at her left hand and snatched off the little moonstone ring she always wore. She shoved the ring into her jeans pocket and glanced up innocently.

"Well, Juliette knows nothing about it," Poco said with assurance. "We've been over it several times. She believes it's an outside job."

"A what?" Georgina and Angela smothered laughs.

"That someone, or some force outside the house, wrote the letter. And her cat instinct tells her it's an unusual being, someone who might be able to see us even though we can't see them."

Angela shivered and gazed around.

"Pilaria!" she whispered. "Maybe it really is the fairy Pilaria, of the Kingdom of the Faeries, Eighth Tribe, Fourth Earth . . ." She paused and listened, as if she'd heard something.

". . . Under the Sun-Star Aravan. Oh, come on!" Georgina exclaimed. "It's all so fishy."

"That may sound bad to you, George," Poco couldn't help putting in, "but to Juliette—" Georgina let out a howl and tossed her head back and forth, as if Poco had finally driven her over the edge.

A door slammed somewhere farther back in

the house. Very soon, loud, angry footsteps could be heard coming down the hall. The figure of Angela's father loomed in the living room doorway.

"*What* is all this silliness that's been going on *all morning*!" he shouted. "I can't stand it *anymore*!"

There was a terrible silence. The three friends froze in their tracks. Juliette tried to escape under a table.

"I-I-I'm sorry, Daddy," Angela finally managed to say. "We didn't know we were bothering you."

Mr. Harrall lowered his head and sighed. Then he looked at them through his little reading glasses and took three tired steps into the room. He was not a young father, not as young as Georgina's father or Poco's by any means. Now, with his scowling face, he seemed fearfully old. And threatening. The girls shrank away from him.

"Well, I'm sorry, too," he said at last. His gaze became sad, suddenly. "I didn't mean to shout. What I meant to do was to ask you, Angela, if you would mind sending your friends home now. I have a little more work to finish this morning. Then I thought the two of us could go out somewhere and . . ." Mr. Harrall stopped and considered. "And do something," he ended lamely.

"Like what?" asked Angela in a doubtful voice.

"Well, I don't know. Something. Your mother will be busy this afternoon and I said I would . . ." His voice trailed off.

Angela sighed and stood up. "Couldn't I just go over to George's house?" she said. "We're working on a project. Then we wouldn't bother you anymore and you could get some more work done this afternoon."

Mr. Harrall shook his head. "No, I promised your mother I'd take care of you. It's all settled, so if you'll just tell your friends"—he peered at Poco as if she were an unfamiliar bug that had somehow crawled up on the couch—"to go home. Right now!" he concluded.

"Okay," Angela said. "Is it all right if I walk them partway? Then I'll come back."

"Fine, fine," her father said. "I'll see you at lunch."

"Okay," replied Angela, and the friends headed with solemn faces for the Harralls' front door.

Chapter Three

Georgina and Poco had run into Angela's father before, so they were not particularly surprised by the scene that ended their investigation of Angela's house. Mr. Harrall was a "nice man" (according to Georgina's mother) and a "big gun in the business world" (Poco's dad), but he was not the sort of father who hung around with children, or cared to know them very well.

Loud noises upset him, and he didn't like the downstairs television going while he was at home. Everyone knew it was because he had to work so hard. He left the house early in the morning and returned late at night, even on weekends. In fact, it had been rather a shock to find him there at all that morning.

"Can you come over tomorrow afternoon?" Georgina asked Angela on her way home. "I know you'll have to check with your mom, but maybe your dad will have work or something."

"I'll see," Angela replied. "I'm sorry he got so mad. He's usually not that bad, but he's been under a lot of stress lately."

"Oh, don't worry," Georgina said. "My dad gets really terrible sometimes. It's something we just have to live with, I guess."

"I guess." Angela came to a halt. "Poco! What are you doing?"

"I think I saw a rabbit go in this bush."

"Well, you can't just lie down on your stomach in the middle of the sidewalk to look!" Georgina cried. "Good grief! You're embarrassing us to death. Here comes a boy from school, too!"

"I'm sorry if I'm embarrassing you, George," Poco said in a voice muffled by leaves. "I just want to find out if—"

"I'll call you tomorrow," Angela told

Georgina quickly. "I'd better get back for lunch." She could foresee a long and difficult struggle coming up. When Poco got onto rabbits, she could be absolutely impossible.

"Sure! Go ahead!" Georgina placed her hands on her hips and looked down furiously. "Now, Poco, listen! I am not going to stand here in the middle of this street and wait while you talk to another rabbit," Angela heard her say as she walked away. "Get up! Get up this minute!"

Whether Poco did get up, or whether she lay on the sidewalk for the next hour being stepped over by passing foot traffic (which she was perfectly capable of doing), Angela never found out. This was because all plans for the following afternoon fell apart. Poco had to go to her grandmother's house for Sunday dinner; Georgina was forced to go with her parents to a museum; and Angela was stuck with her family at home. Not until Monday morning, during music class, were the friends able to meet again. And what Angela reported then, in whispers between songs, instantly erased all other thoughts from their minds.

"I got another letter!"

"You did?"

"Yes! On the mantelpiece again."

"From Pilaria?"

"Yes! But I hadn't even written her."

"You hadn't?"

"No!"

This brief burst of communication was interrupted by that most dreary and endless of songs, "Puff, the Magic Dragon." Poco, who had a good voice, sang loudly.

"Is it written in purple ink?" Georgina whispered when the song was finally done.

"Yes!"

"Gold dust?"

"Yes!"

"On the same paper, tied with gold thread?"

"Yes, exactly the same."

"What does it say?"

At this moment, Mrs. Henderson, the music teacher, came down hard with both hands on the piano, and the conversation was drowned out by unearthly wails of "Oh-oh say ken yoo seeeee?" This is one of the most impossible songs to sing ever written and requires huge gulps of air to get through the lines. Georgina and Angela were so dizzy by the end that they could only fall back in their folding chairs and wait for the next song to be announced.

"Tell us at lunch!" Poco leaned over to say—just in time, because three seconds later she was chosen by Mrs. Henderson to come up to the front of the room and practice a solo for the fall concert.

It turned out to be that old screecher "Over the Rainbow." Poco led off the verses in a clear, high voice.

The rest of them came in on the fluttery parts, sounding, as Georgina hissed to Angela, like a lot of idiot birds taking off into the air.

"How can someone so little sing so loud?" Angela whispered back. There was really no answer to this, and Georgina did not bother to reply. They were both exhausted from music by this time and slumped down and sang in tones inaudible to the human ear for the rest of the class.

It was no good having Angela tell them about the new letter. Georgina and Poco would have to see it if they were going to believe.

"Of course I didn't bring it to school!" Angela said at lunch. "It's much too precious to carry around."

So the friends walked to Angela's house after school, and when Georgina and Poco had called their mothers to say where they were, everyone went to Angela's room and sat on her bed.

Angela had hidden the new letter in a shoe box in her closet. Now, sitting cross-legged on the bed, she unfurled it with cautious fingers, at every moment expecting the gold dust to fly out. And suddenly, poof! It did! Georgina reached for it, but too late. The dust vanished almost as soon as it hit the air, like a puff of smoke. It was the oddest thing.

Even odder was the letter. Angela read the page of beautiful purple writing out loud while the others hung over her shoulder following the words.

"ANGELA:

I, Pilaria, known also as the Gray-Eyed Faerie, salute you and beg for your ear. Your letter was a great wonder to me, who has had no friend in the human world for many years. I had forgotten how pleasant it can be to talk with a mortal being, especially one who is a child with such interesting thoughts as you. Chocolate boxes that never empty! Old happinesses like these have long been lost to me. Will you tell me of other wishes that you have? I would like to know you and your secrets better.

Respectfully yours,
PILARIA
of the Kingdom of the Faeries,
Eighth Tribe, Fourth Earth,
Under the Sun-Star Aravan,
May It Shine on Our Land
Forever and Ever"

When Angela had finished reading, she looked up at her friends with such glowing eyes that neither could doubt she believed in the letter absolutely.

"Look at it!" she cried, holding the page up. "It comes from another world. I know it! I can feel it! Pilaria is real. And she is lonely for a friend."

"How long do fairies live, do you think?" Poco asked. "From this letter, it sounds like she's been around for hundreds of years."

"I don't know," Angela said, "but I can imagine that she would sort of run out of friends if she lived long enough."

"Wait a minute!" Georgina interrupted. "None of this adds up. If Pilaria has been hanging around all these years, why did she never try to write to Angela before? She could have left a letter on the mantelpiece anytime in the last nine years. Instead, she waits until Angela writes a dumb letter about a box of chocolates that does something completely impossible, and then she starts asking to be her friend. This doesn't sound fake to you?"

"No!" said Angela.

Poco looked less sure. "But who else could be doing it?" she asked Georgina. "And why? And what about the gold dust? It's strange, you have to admit."

Georgina shook her head. "I'm not saying it isn't strange. I'm saying we haven't investigated well enough yet. For instance, how do these letters get onto Angela's mantelpiece?"

"Someone puts them there?" Poco ventured.

"Right! And our next investigation will be to see who."

"But I know who!" cried Angela. "It's Pilaria!"

"What I mean is," said Georgina, looking thoroughly annoyed, "we are going to spy and find out what the person who calls herself Pilaria looks like. Maybe she'll look like a gray-eyed faerie, or maybe she'll look like"—Georgina paused and glanced coolly at Angela—"your mother," she ended.

"My mother is not writing these letters!"

Angela protested. "She has terrible penmanship. And anyway, she's not interested in things like this. She works part-time in a bank, you know. In fact, no one in my family even knows about these letters, so please don't tell them. No one knows I wrote the first letter. I put it out late at night, and found the answer early the next morning. Listen, the people in my family hardly have time to do all the things they're supposed to do. These letters aren't from them."

"Well, we'll see, won't we?" Georgina replied smugly.

"Only if I say so!" said Angela, showing a bit of angry flush.

"Well, Angela Harrall! I think you're being absolutely—"

Poco jumped into the conversation at this moment, and Georgina never did finish her sentence, which was just as well.

"I am beginning to think," Poco declared, "that Juliette might be Pilaria after all. She seemed to be hiding something when I talked to her last time. Cats have connections with the spirit world, you know. Some people believe they are really the eyes of the dead that have come back to watch us. Maybe Pilaria is a dead person."

"Poco! That's ridiculous!" exclaimed Angela

and Georgina in the same breath. Then they looked at each other and burst out laughing.

"Now I'll never be able to trust that cat again!" Angela cried. "I'll always be wondering whose horrible old eyes are looking at me."

Even Poco began to laugh at this, and the three girls went into an absolute storm of giggles and rolled off the bed and around on the floor. Soon, several knocks sounded on Angela's door. They all sat up in terror of its being Angela's father on a surprise visit home. But it was only Mrs. Harrall saying that she was going to the store and would they all like to come and get ice-cream cones on the way? She was the nicest mother. She seemed to know what the friends wanted to do even before they knew it themselves.

"Ice cream!"

"Oh yes!"

"We can work on our spy plan tomorrow afternoon. At my house," Georgina whispered to Angela and Poco as they got into Mrs. Harrall's car.

So it was agreed. And not a moment too soon, for that night something even more amazing happened in the Harrall house.

Chapter Four

Angela thought at first that she would not tell her friends. Real magic is a fragile thing. One rude gust of outside air and it can fly to pieces. One cold eye, one unbelieving word, and the most marvelous constructions may collapse and turn to nothing.

Angela felt protective of the magic that had risen up so unexpectedly in her house. Why it had come she could not begin to guess. That it really was there, in the shape of a lonely, old-fashioned fairy, she knew beyond doubt. There are some things a person knows, no matter how impossible they seem to others.

By lunchtime, however, Angela was so swelled up with her secret that she could hardly eat. After lunch, she drew the friends together on the playground and, with a sigh, gave in and allowed herself to speak.

"You saw Pilaria?" Georgina shrieked.

"Yes."

"I don't believe it."

"Well, I did."

"Was she very little?" Poco asked.

"I don't know. Maybe."

"You don't know!" Georgina frowned. "I thought you said you saw her."

"I did."

"Well . . . ?"

"I didn't see her body," Angela said. "I'm sure it was there, but I didn't see that part."

"'That part'?" Georgina looked furious. "What other part is there?"

"I saw her light," Angela said simply, and Poco, whose head had been somewhat below the others' because she was so short, stood up suddenly on her toes so as not to miss the next words.

"It was late last night," whispered Angela. "I made myself wake up. Then I crept downstairs with my flashlight and left Pilaria a note on the mantelpiece. It was just a stupid note saying that I had gotten her letters and wanted to be friends if she wanted to be. After I left it, I went back upstairs and shut the flashlight off. But then I had to go to the bathroom. When I came out, I thought I heard something, so I went to the top of the stairs and looked down. That's when I saw her."

"What exactly did you see?" Georgina asked.

"I saw a strange round ball of light come flickering along the downstairs hall," Angela said, her voice quivering a bit. "It went into the living room, and I could see by the shadows it made in the hall that it went across to the fireplace. There was not one sound, but the light fluttered and stopped and fluttered again. Then it came out of the living room in a sort of blinding flash, and whisk! it disappeared."

"Whisk?" repeated Georgina, with a disbelieving look.

"That's what it sounded like," Angela said. "Whisk! Then she was gone."

Poco dropped down off her toes and gazed thoughtfully at the ground.

"I suppose all that fluttering was her wings?" she asked, glancing up.

"I think so," Angela said.

"And the whisk was when she flew away?"

"Oh no," Angela said. "The whisk was when she disappeared and went back into her own world, the one that's invisible to us."

Poco considered this for a moment.

"Where was Juliette?" she asked Angela.

"In the kitchen, I suppose. Under the radiator, where she always sleeps."

"But you aren't sure?"

"No," Angela said. "Except I don't think it was Juliette. Or a dead person. I wasn't scared at all. I was happy!"

"What about your note?" Poco asked.

"It was gone this morning when I looked. Pilaria took it."

Georgina turned her back abruptly and looked off across the playground, where swarms of children were running back and forth and yelling. Then she turned to face her friends again.

"Can we spend the night on Friday?" she asked Angela.

"I don't know. Maybe, if my dad isn't there. I'll have to ask."

"See if we can," Georgina said. "Then maybe you could write another note and get the fairy to come back."

Angela's eyes narrowed at this suggestion.

"I don't think so," she said. "Something like

that can't be planned. I don't like the idea of spying."

Georgina shifted her weight impatiently. She opened her mouth to speak again, but Poco beat her to it.

"How about if we just came to spend the night?" she asked Angela. "Not to spy or anything. We would just be there with you, and if anything happened, okay, and if not, well, that would be okay, too."

Angela thought this over for about half a minute.

"I guess that would be all right," she said at last.

"Yay, Angela! Great! Fantastic!" Georgina and Poco jumped for joy.

"Don't forget, I have to ask my mother," Angela warned them. "If my father is going to be there, you probably can't come. He's been getting worse and worse lately. Even my mother hardly dares to talk to him."

"Well, ask her!" said Georgina. "Do it tonight so she can't say it's the last minute."

"That's right," Poco exclaimed. "My mom is always saying we can't do things because we didn't plan to do them at least three days before. It's completely crazy. If we suddenly want to do something, why do we need to plan that we want to do it, and then wait around for three days for the plan to start?"

The friends were about to begin a full-scale discussion of this weird behavior when the bell rang, signaling the end of recess.

"Do you still want to come over to my house after school?" Georgina asked the other two, as they all ran across the playground.

"Okay," puffed Angela.

"Can I hold your hamster?" asked Poco. "He's an interesting person to talk to when he isn't running around on that squeaky wheel of his."

The next two days passed slowly for the group. The weather turned bad. A ferocious storm let loose torrents of rain, followed by wind and hail, more rain, and finally a tornado watch that scared traffic off the streets—until the sun came out and an all-clear message was broadcast over the radio.

This took place late Thursday afternoon while the friends huddled in Poco's kitchen. They were supposed to be baking chocolate chip cookies but, feeling rather nervous about the tornado, they had ended up eating most of the cookie dough.

"This is ridiculous," Georgina said. "There's

only enough dough left for about three cookies. Let's just finish it off. Then we won't have to wait around for anything to bake."

"I'm sort of full, anyway," Poco said.

"Me, too." Georgina scraped up one last wooden spoonful of dough and offered it to Angela. "Do you want the last bit?" she asked.

"No, thank you." Angela sat back in her chair and sighed.

"What is the matter with you today?" Georgina asked. "You've been in a terrible mood ever since we got here."

"I don't know. Nothing."

"Has your mother said yet whether we can spend the night tomorrow?"

"No."

"Well, what's the problem?" Georgina demanded. "Either we can or we can't. Why won't she decide?"

"It's not that simple," Angela said, sinking down another inch in the kitchen chair. "Nothing is simple in my family."

"That is no excuse," said Georgina. "Nothing is simple in anyone's family. My little sister screams all night from bad dreams, and my father got his hand caught in the mower. And Poco's brother crashed their station wagon into their garage door and now Mrs. Lambert has gotten fired from her job, so they can't afford to get anything fixed."

"Ssh!" whispered Poco, looking over her shoulder. "My mother doesn't consider it being fired. She's just staying home until the company finds some more money to pay her."

"Well, whatever!" Georgina looked thoroughly disgusted. "Things are tough for everybody."

Poco leaned close to Angela. "Is it your father?" she asked softly.

"I guess so."

"He doesn't want us to come?"

"Oh no. He doesn't know anything about it. He doesn't care what I do as long I don't bother him. It's my mom. She's been sort of down lately."

"Why?"

"I don't know, but my dad doesn't stay with her at night anymore. He's started sleeping downstairs in his office."

The friends were silent for a little while after this revelation. They all knew people whose parents were divorced.

"Well, it doesn't necessarily mean anything," Georgina said finally. Poco nodded.

"I know." Angela lowered her head. "He

asked me to go bowling with him this Saturday. Alone. Without my brother or anyone. I said I didn't want to."

"What happened then?"

"Nothing. He just looked mad and went away without saying anything."

Georgina took the empty cookie-dough bowl to the sink and ran water into it.

"Listen, Angela. Don't worry about things like that," she said over the running water. "Parents get into fights. You can't let it bother you. You've got to carry on with your own plans. Ask your mother again if we can spend the night on Friday. It sounds like she forgot to decide anything because she got upset about your dad."

This was good advice, as it turned out. Mrs. Harrall really had forgotten that Angela had asked and, when she was reminded, agreed to the sleepover immediately.

"I'm so sorry!" she exclaimed. "It went completely out of my mind. Your brother is going hiking this weekend, so it's a good time to have everyone. I'll call Mrs. Lambert and Mrs. Rusk tonight, and then Poco and Georgina can bring their overnight bags to school and walk home with you tomorrow afternoon. Will that be all right?"

She peered anxiously at Angela. Rather too anxiously, Angela thought, with a jab of fear.

"Will Dad be here?" she asked her mother.

"I don't believe he will," Mrs. Harrall replied in such a cold and final tone that Angela knew not to ask any more about it.

So everything was arranged, and Poco and Georgina began to feel little streaks of excitement about being in Angela's house. Pilaria had not left anything on the mantelpiece all week. She had not answered Angela's letter. Did this mean that perhaps she would appear when they were there?

"Personally, I have my doubts about this whole thing," Georgina told Poco in the hall before school on Friday morning. "But I'm bringing my mother's camera just in case something happens."

"Angela won't like that," Poco warned. "She'll say you shouldn't take pictures of magic beings."

"Angela can't control everything," Georgina said. "Besides, I'm going to hide the camera. She won't know I have it. Unless you tell her." Georgina shot a suspicious glance at Poco. "And if you do, I promise that I will never, ever, in my entire life, speak to you again."

"George! Why would I tell? You don't have to be so snappish," Poco said. "You are worse than a pack of llamas."

"Of what?"

"Llamas," Poco repeated. "Haven't you ever talked to one? They refuse to trust anyone and are always snapping at people because they think they're being tricked. Of course, when llamas snap, it isn't with words but with big, sharp teeth, so it's best to keep out of their way."

Georgina was completely infuriated by this remark, but she bit her lip and kept back the cutting reply that sprang to mind. What else could she do? One word and she would have looked more like a nasty llama than ever.

Chapter Five

A golden autumn sun was shining down full and strong as the three friends walked together along the sidewalk to Angela's house that afternoon. All signs of the bad weather had disappeared, and with it had gone Angela's gloomy mood. She was as happy and chirpy as a spring robin, already beginning to play the role of hostess before her home had even come into view.

"We have three kinds of soda—orange, Coke, and root beer," she announced, prancing in front of the others. "And popcorn if anyone wants it. Which no one probably will because we also have"—she paused for dramatic effect—"ice-cream sandwiches!"

"Mmm."

"Yum."

Poco and Georgina seemed quieter than usual. They tramped heavily along. Both were carrying stuffed knapsacks on their backs. Georgina's, in particular, looked about ready to burst, Angela noticed.

"What on earth have you got in there, George!" she cried out. Luckily, she did not really expect an answer. A minute later she was describing the things they might do that afternoon: leaf raking in the backyard, video games in the den, Ping-Pong on the third floor. The Harralls' house was bigger than the Lamberts' or the Rusks', thanks to Mr. Harrall's business success. It had many beautiful rooms and soft couches and velvety rugs. Angela even had a small TV by her bed.

Today, however, these delights seemed not to interest Angela's friends as much as they had in the past.

No sooner was Georgina in the house than she went to the mantelpiece in the living room and stared at it. She walked down the hall where Angela had seen the fairy's light and noticed that the den, the kitchen, and the dining room opened off it. Beyond this cluster of rooms, farther to the back, were a family room and Mr. Harrall's dark, leathery office. The second floor could be reached by a back stairway that came up from the family room, as well as by the front stairway, Georgina noted.

"Can I look at Pilaria's letters again?" she asked Angela. "Does gold dust still fly out whenever you unroll them?"

"Not as much," Angela had to admit. "I've opened them so many times."

Poco was in deep conference with Juliette by now, though few words were actually being exchanged. They lay on their stomachs on the dining-room carpet, almost nose to nose, staring at each other. Every once in a while Poco would say, "Ve-r-r-y interesting." And Juliette would twitch her tail.

This was the sort of thing that drove Georgina absolutely wild, so Angela took her outside into the backyard. The leaves were just beginning to fall. There weren't really enough to make a decent leaf pile yet.

"How does it feel to have real magic come into your house?" Georgina asked, looking around the yard with hard, practical eyes.

"It feels . . . okay," Angela replied in a guarded tone. "It feels like I have a new friend."

"Why is it we've never seen or heard about fairies coming into people's houses before?" Georgina asked. "Except in fairy tales, which don't count. We should have heard more about it if such things really happened."

"Not necessarily," Angela said. "In real life, real magic happens only once in a while. Afterward, we forget we saw it, or people tell us we're crazy so we don't believe what we saw anymore. Then we're surprised all over again when it happens another time."

"Angela, you made that up just this minute, didn't you!" Georgina said in disgust. "You've never had that idea ever before in your life."

"That's right," Angela said, with an odd little smile. "I never did think anything like that before. I think it's true, though. Maybe I'm beginning to come under Pilaria's spell."

"Oh, come on! Now Pilaria is making spells?"

"No, it's not like that," Angela replied. "But lately I've had the strangest feeling that she's near me. She's around the house, just out of sight. I talk to her sometimes, in my room, in case she's there. And you know, it sometimes seems that she is listening. I think she is interested in me."

"Good grief! You sound as nutty as Poco!" Georgina exclaimed. She turned and marched off toward a distant clump of trees in the yard, hoping that Angela wouldn't follow, which she did not. The whole situation was so infuriating.

"Angela's letters are being written by somebody who lives close to Angela," Georgina muttered to herself as she walked. But by whom? She couldn't think. Angela's mother didn't know anything about the letters. Anyone could see that from the way she acted. Angela's brother, Martin, had no interest in his sister. He was six years older and played a lot of sports. Angela's father was never home and hardly spoke to her when he was. He always looked upset whenever Angela was around. Could Juliette have been right when she said it was "an outside job"?

"Wait a minute!" Georgina said out loud in the middle of the clump of trees. "I do *not* believe that Angela's fat old cat can talk!"

Nevertheless, and against her better judgment, she found herself walking back across the yard toward the house. Perhaps by now, Poco had picked up some other bit of information from Juliette. It was a ridiculous idea, utterly impossible and out of the question, but Georgina could think of nowhere else to turn.

"Juliette is upset," Poco reported, when Georgina found her upstairs. She was unrolling her sleeping bag in Angela's room, unpacking her overnight bag and settling in. Poco was not really an overnight sort of person. She felt nervous about being away from home, even with friends, and liked to arrange things around herself in a special, familiar way.

"Why is Juliette upset?" asked Georgina, who could have slept on a battleship as long as she was in charge of it.

"Because she doesn't feel happy."

Georgina frowned. "I know that. But why?"

"She says the air currents in this house are blocked."

"And what does she mean by that?"

"How should I know?" Poco began to look upset herself. She opened her overnight bag and removed a sweatshirt without looking at Georgina.

"Well, does it have anything to do with the letters?" Georgina demanded.

"I don't know!"

"Why not?"

Poco glared at her. Georgina was acting like a chief of police, asking a lot of impossible questions and then getting angry when she didn't like the answers.

"Look, George. I'm just telling you what Juliette said, okay? I can't read her mind!"

"This is ridiculous!" Georgina fumed. "We

are getting nowhere. That's what happens when you try to talk to a cat!"

"That is a completely unfair thing to say!" shouted Poco, who almost never shouted.

"But it's true!"

"People like you will never understand!" Poco yelled.

"And people like you will never find out anything about anything that's important!" Georgina shrieked back.

"Ssh!" hissed Angela, coming suddenly into the room. "What is the matter with you? My mother is wondering what's going on."

Poco and Georgina glowered at each other and turned their backs.

"I guess we're all a little nervous," Angela said. "Let's pull ourselves together. It might be important for tonight. Look what I've done: written Pilaria another letter."

Both friends turned around at this and noticed the piece of paper she held in her hand.

"Listen," said Angela, and she sat down on her bed and read the following, out loud:

"To Pilaria, of the Kingdom of the Faeries, Eighth Tribe, Fourth Earth, Under the Sun-Star Aravan, May It Shine on Your Land Forever and Ever:

Hi! Did you get my last letter? I was hoping you'd write back. If you want to, that is. I have some questions.

1. *Where do you live?*
2. *How old are you?*
3. *Will you live forever?*
4. *Do you still grant wishes like in the old days?*

You don't have to answer if you don't want to. I know how busy you must be.

Respecfully yours,
ANGELA HARRALL"

"Oh, Angela, that is very good," Poco said when she had finished. "Are you going to leave it on the mantelpiece?"

"Yes."

"Do you think Pilaria might answer to-night?"

"I don't know. I didn't want to say 'Please answer tonight.' You can't tell someone like that what to do," Angela said, glancing at Georgina. "I tried to hint to Pilaria that I wanted to hear from her soon. So, who knows? She might come."

Georgina nodded and leaned forward. "You

spelled 'respectfully' wrong," she said, pointing. "There's a *t* after the *c*."

They all leaned over the letter while Angela took out her pen and put in the *t*.

"I think we should set up a night-watch system," Georgina said then. "It won't do any good if Pilaria comes and we're all asleep."

Angela looked as if she was about to protest against any unnatural systems, but Georgina added, quickly, "It won't be to spy. We don't want to hurt her. In a way it will be so we can protect her and be her friend. We could do that a lot better if we knew what sort of being she is."

Angela still appeared doubtful, so Poco said, "I've been thinking that maybe Pilaria wants us to see her. She controls her invisibleness, right? If she didn't want to be seen, why would she be going around the house in a great beam of light?"

"Hmmm," Angela said.

"From what she said in her letter, she's mostly kept herself invisible before," Poco went on. "For years and years. I think Pilaria wants to come into our world, now. I think she's interested in Angela and wants Angela to see her."

This was a wonderful and amazing thought, and Angela had to agree that it might be true.

Not more than fifteen minutes later, a night-watch plan had been arranged.

Angela was to take the first watch, which would start shortly after Mrs. Harrall went to bed that night. The best place to watch from was the top of the front stairs. It provided a good view of the downstairs hall, and of the doorway leading to the living room. Also, the person on watch would be able to fetch the others quickly if Pilaria appeared.

At 1:00 A.M., Georgina would take over and be on duty until 4:00 A.M. Poco would take the last watch.

"I get up early, anyway," she said. "It's the best time to talk to birds. They're the kind of people who like to hop out of bed and get things done before breakfast."

"Oh, really," muttered Georgina, but without much force. The idea that they might, this very night, catch sight of Pilaria—whatever she might be—was beginning to seem awesome even to her. Indeed, all three friends were unusually quiet during dinner with Angela's mother that evening.

"I hope I am not as boring as you are making me feel!" poor Mrs. Harrall said during dessert. "I've tried every subject I can think of, but no one seems interested in a word I say. I suppose you must have something on your minds."

"Oh, we do," Angela replied gratefully.

"It isn't you," Poco said.

"Dinner was great," Georgina added.

Then, because Mrs. Harrall looked a little sad and tired, the friends helped her with the dishes and joked around to cheer her up.

"You have the nicest mother," Poco whispered to Angela later, as they were going to watch television in the family room. "I feel so sorry about your dad."

Angela made no answer to this, however, and very soon the group was wrapped up again in their exciting plan for the night.

Chapter Six

Up until about midnight, the friends were full of energy and could not even think of going to bed. This was supposed to be Angela's watch, but they were all so eager to see Pilaria that everyone crowded together at the top of the stairs, whispering frantically.

Mrs. Harrall poked her head out of her door once and asked them, please, not to stay up too late. Afterward, from her room, came the soft strains of a classical music station. A little later, her light went off.

"That's it. Now we don't have to worry about her for the rest of the night. She's a heavy sleeper," Angela told the group when she came back from checking.

Even so, they were careful to keep their voices quiet. The night seemed to require it. They turned off the light in the hall. Gradually, they grew less fidgety and began to stop whispering. The silence of the Harralls' big house swam in around them, and each friend leaned back and thought her own thoughts. But everyone kept an eye on the downstairs hall, where the shadows seemed sometimes to creep forward, and sometimes to shrink back. It was hard to tell what was real and what their minds were inventing.

A short while after midnight, Poco yawned and said she was going to bed. Georgina declared that she would stay up with Angela until the beginning of her own watch. When one o'clock came, Angela decided to stay up with Georgina for a while. But very soon, a heavy drowsiness settled over her, and she went, reluctantly, to join Poco in the bedroom.

By one-thirty, Georgina was the only person on the stairs. She sat huddled in a blanket on the top step. The air in the house had turned chilly. Outside, the noise of a lone car passing in the street came through the front windows. Georgina rubbed her eyes. Darkness had spread over the floors and up the walls like a black flood. Below, in the hall, certain shadows seemed to press forward again. She began to feel that something was watching her. A strange squeak echoed up the stairs. Georgina's heart jumped. She leaned forward and peered into the blackness.

But time went by and nothing happened. She sat back on the step again. Her eyes kept wanting to close. She put her head against the wall and shut them for just a moment. The last time she remembered looking at her watch, it was 2:05.

"Psst! Georgina!"

She woke with a jolt and saw that Angela was crouched beside her. "Look down in the hall," Angela said.

A faint light was coming from the living room.

"Pilaria's here. I'm going to get Poco," Angela whispered. She disappeared, and Georgina felt a sudden rush of fear at being left alone with the unknown thing below.

Poco and Angela came back almost immediately, though.

"Incredible!" Poco gasped when she saw the light coming from the living room.

It made a dim rectangle on the hall rug, too weak for a lamp or even a flashlight. The outline of the door frame was barely visible. From time to time, the light wavered and grew dimmer. Then it brightened again. Fluttered. Thin rustling sounds made their way up the stairs to the group's straining ears. There was no question that something was there in that room.

"I'm going down," Georgina breathed.

"No!" Angela shook her head.

"I want to see what it is!"

"No!"

"Angela! Someone has to look."

"Let's just wait," Angela whispered. "I'm afraid we'll scare her and she'll never come back."

"Don't you want us to see Pilaria?" Georgina asked angrily. "It always seems as if you're trying to keep us from getting too close."

"No, of course not!"

"Well, it seems that way."

"Pilaria wrote to me. I'm the one who should see her!" Angela said.

"*You* go down and look then," Georgina hissed in exasperation. "Someone has got to do it. We must see what she looks like."

"All right!"

Angela stood up slowly. She was wearing a summer nightgown with short sleeves. As she stepped past Poco, their bare arms brushed.

"Angela, you're cold as ice!"

"I'm all right."

"Don't go if you feel too scared," Poco whispered. "We don't have to look."

"Yes, we do!" Georgina exclaimed.

"It's all right," Angela said. "I'll go down slowly so Pilaria doesn't hear me. You two stay here."

While her friends watched, Angela began to creep down the stairs. At first she held on to the banister to keep her balance. But it was loose around its poles and creaked. She let go and reached for the wall on the other side. With her palm pressed against it, she descended one step, then another. The thick carpet on the stairway muffled her tread. Below her, the glow in the living room began to flutter again, and Poco and Georgina saw shadows dancing on the rug just inside the doorway.

Both of them were shivering a little by now, half from cold, half from nervousness. Angela looked shaky, too, but she continued to go down. When she came to the bottom step, she turned and glanced back at them. Her face was so white that it looked like a sick person's.

Stop! Poco wanted to call out. *You don't have to go!*

But beside her, Georgina was waving Angela on impatiently. "Go!" she was mouthing. "Hurry up! Now!"

At first (Poco was right), Angela had been afraid of seeing Pilaria. Or perhaps she was afraid of not seeing her. At the top of the stairs, her courage had suddenly fled and her usually reliable legs had started to shiver. A magic being in the living room! It was too wonderful to believe. What if the magic should fail? What if none of it were true?

But now—Angela gazed up the stairs at her friends—now that she had come all the way down, a great excitement began to rise in her. She stepped toward the lighted doorway with confident eyes. Pilaria wanted to be seen. Poco had said so. She was interested in Angela and would not mind if she looked. Angela approached the living room quietly, her bare feet cushioned by hall carpet. When she reached the doorway, she drew in her breath and peeked around the corner.

All she could see in the beginning was a dazzling glow in the center of the mantelpiece. It was exactly as if someone had lit a small fire there and gone away, leaving it to burn. Several seconds passed before Angela realized that the glow was in motion. It was moving around in a circle, waving and flickering, and seemed to be made up of many wings, not a single pair. Angela squinted and peered.

"Pilaria?" she whispered, leaning into the room.

There was no answer, but the glow burned brighter. Its light surged in warm waves through the room. It caught the edge of a picture frame, the china cheek of a bowl, the shaft of a lamp. Each flared up briefly, then blended back into the gloom. On the mantelpiece, the fairy's wings flickered and glowed, and dimmed. They moved more slowly. A faint rustling sound came to Angela's ear. She took two steps forward and paused. Behind her, in the hall, she heard Poco and Georgina coming cautiously down the stairs.

"Pilaria? Is that you?" Angela asked. "What are you doing?" She was about to creep closer to the amazing being, when a terrible uproar broke out in back of her.

"Stop! Where are you going?" a voice bellowed in the hall. Heavy footsteps shook the floor and came to a halt at the bottom of the stairs.

"We are just waiting here," Angela heard Poco say in a frightened voice. "For Angela. She's in there."

"Where!"

"In the living room."

Even before Poco had finished answering, Angela's father was rushing into the room. He stormed toward Angela like a furious, dark monster, grabbed her by the arm, and pulled her through the door.

"Angela Harrall! What are you doing up?"

Angela's hands flew to her mouth. She trembled all over and could not speak.

"Who are these children? Your friends? What are they doing here?" Mr. Harrall shook Angela's shoulder fiercely. "Where is your mother? Asleep upstairs?"

Angela nodded with teary eyes.

"William? Is that you?" Mrs. Harrall's voice floated down from upstairs at just that moment.

"Yes! And I've caught Angela here. Still up at this hour! With her friends running wild all over the house!"

"No we weren't!" Georgina protested. "We were just on the stairs!" Mr. Harrall glared at her and let go of Angela, whom he had been holding by the shoulder like a criminal all this time. She backed away from him and went to stand with Poco and Georgina.

"William! What is happening down there?" Angela's mother called. "Are the girls . . . ?"

"Yes! Wide-awake. Running around down here, out of control!"

Mrs. Harrall leaned over the upstairs banister and looked down at the small, quaking group below. "Oh, Angela," she said in a disappointed tone. "I particularly asked you not to stay up too late. Do you realize that it's past three o'clock in the morning?"

Angela still could find no voice for a reply. Her eyes were wider than Poco had ever seen them. And they were filled with tears only just now beginning to overflow onto her cheeks.

"It's all right, William. I didn't know you were coming home tonight. I'm sorry they bothered you," Mrs. Harrall said to her husband. "I suppose it's asking too much to let me know your schedule in advance?"

"I told you I'd be home tonight," Angela's father replied angrily. "Several times, as I remember."

"Well, I remember none of them!" Mrs. Harrall snapped back. "Come on up, girls." She motioned to them. "My goodness. I certainly am surprised at you all! And after I specially asked you to be good about settling down . . . "

So the friends slunk upstairs to bed. No one dared to look back to see what had become of Pilaria. Mr. Harrall was standing in the middle of the hall scowling at every step they took. And Mrs. Harrall was frowning and ordering them under the covers.

"And no talking! Or I shall have to separate you," she said in a cross voice as she closed the bedroom door. It was quite unlike her.

For a long time after this, there was no sound in the room, except for Angela's little sniffs as she cried into her pillow. The friends lay rigid as boards in their sleeping bags and listened to the angry silence of the night. Poco was close to tears herself. She wished that she had never agreed to stay overnight and wondered where Juliette was at that moment. It would have been so nice to have a soft body to hold.

Finally, since Angela's sniffs seemed to be turning into more of a rushing stream, Georgina sat up and spoke in a whisper.

"Angela! What did you see?"

Angela didn't answer immediately. She took a minute to gather herself. To her credit,

Georgina didn't push her, for once. She sat still and waited, and pretty soon Angela cleared her throat and said, "I saw Pilaria again. She was all lit up."

"Where?"

"On the mantelpiece. I think she was picking up my letter."

The friends lay quietly, considering this. Then Poco sat up and leaned close to the others.

"Could you see if she left you anything?" she asked.

Angela shook her head. In the dark, it sounded like a low, sad rustle. "I think everything is over," she said. "Pilaria won't ever come again after tonight."

"What do you mean?" Georgina asked.

"She won't, that's all, because it isn't safe here. This is not a good house. This is a stupid, hateful house that could never believe in anything!"

Angela uttered this last sentence so bitterly that the friends were shocked. They knew she was speaking of something more than fairy belief.

"Maybe Pilaria will come again," Georgina said gently. "Maybe she'll feel sad for you. You never know with magic beings. Sometimes they are scared away, but sometimes they decide to come out all the more."

These were such unlikely words to hear from Georgina, who had been so suspicious of Pilaria before, that her friends looked at her in surprise.

"Do you think so?" Angela asked doubtfully. "Oh, George, do you really think that?"

"Why not?" Georgina replied. "Pilaria likes you. She let you see her, didn't she? She wouldn't turn her back and walk out on you now."

After this, all three friends lay down under their covers with a much happier feeling. And quite soon, they had fallen asleep. All over the Harrall house, a new, peaceful silence rose up, and the air seemed to drift more easily through the rooms. Under her radiator, Juliette lifted her head and glanced about with her wise Siamese eyes. Then she pulled her tail close, began a satisfied purr, and settled down to sleep.

Chapter Seven

Georgina and Poco were still asleep the next morning when Angela burst through the door of her bedroom with a loud cry. She had been downstairs in the living room and, "Guess what!" she shrieked. "Look what I found!"

This was not a nice way to wake people up, especially people who had gone to bed at three the night before. Or was it three-thirty? Georgina covered her ears and rolled away. Poco groaned and pulled the sleeping bag over her head. Angela, however, would not be put off.

"Get up!" she screeched. "This is very important! Pilaria wants to go on. She has left another letter!"

These words had more effect. Sweeping their tangled hair from their faces, the friends tried to sit up and show some interest in the world.

"Good grief!" Angela declared. "You are taking forever to even open your eyes. I think I'll go have breakfast."

No, no, no. The friends were awake.

"As awake as we ever will be at this hour," Georgina mumbled.

"Read us the letter," Poco yawned. "We can't wait to hear it."

Angela sat cross-legged on her bed and held up the new letter, which was rolled and tied with the same gold thread as the others.

"Wait!" Georgina ordered. She crawled over and cupped her hands under the letter. "Okay, ready."

Angela began, very carefully, to unroll the paper.

Poof! The gold dust flew out and shimmered down through the air. Georgina did everything she could to get her hands around it, but without success. The dust vanished as she touched it and left no sign of itself on the blanket below.

"It's like fireworks on the Fourth of July,"

Poco said. "They burst out in a big shining cloud, and then, a second later, they completely disappear. No one ever sees fireworks come down."

Georgina frowned and examined her hands on both sides.

"Listen to this!" said Angela, who now had the letter open.

"Angela:

I, Pilaria, known also as the Gray-Eyed Faerie, send friendship and love in this time of trouble. Your letters made me happy and I will try to answer your questions. You asked where I live. My world is invisible to you, and would seem strange if you could see it. Here there are no colors, only dark grays and browns. The people go about with stiff faces, and few can say what is really on their minds. We faeries have fallen on hard times in recent years. Though we do not speak of it to one another, we often long for the bright, merry days of our past in the First and Second Earths.

I have forgotten my age, but feel it is very great. My power to grant wishes has lately grown weak. I am sorry.

Will you write me more about yourself?

Respectfully yours,
Pilaria
of the Kingdom of the Faeries,
Eighth Tribe, Fourth Earth,
Under the Sun-Star Aravan,
May It Shine on Our Land
Forever and Ever"

"Oh! That is so sad!" exclaimed Angela, as she allowed the letter to roll itself back up. Like the others, it seemed to prefer privacy. "I never thought fairies lived such hard lives!"

"Well, they didn't always," Poco said. "Pilaria says she used to be happy. I wonder what happened."

"One thing that happened is that a lot of time went by," Georgina said in her practical voice. "Did you notice how Pilaria talks about First and Second Earths in this letter? And then, down on the bottom, she signs it with 'Fourth Earth.' It makes you wonder if other sorts of worlds existed on our planet before we came along."

"That would certainly explain some strange things that Juliette has said to me," Poco declared. "She keeps talking about the eight lives she's lived in other times and other places."

"A cat's nine lives—oh, please!" Georgina

rolled her eyes. She got up and started to get dressed.

"Anyway," Angela said, "I guess Pilaria wasn't very upset by my father last night. She doesn't mention a thing about it."

"What *did* you see last night, anyway?" Poco asked her. "You haven't really told us yet."

Angela lay down on her bed and propped her head up with one hand. In a low voice, she began to tell about the extraordinary light she had seen burning on the mantelpiece when she entered the living room. She explained how, at first, she had mistaken the glow for a small fire, and then it had appeared to be many wings flying in a circle. At last she had realized that the light came from one pair of wings, and when she had spoken the light had burned brighter, so she knew that Pilaria had heard her.

"What color was the light?" Georgina inquired. "Red? Silver? White, like a light bulb?"

"Oh no," Angela said. "It was golden. Like the magic dust and the gold thread around the letters. Pilaria is gold colored all over. That's the sort of being she is."

Georgina's old suspicious gaze blinked on when she heard this. "And what happened when your father came in? Did her golden light just go off?" she asked.

"I don't know."

"You mean you didn't notice?"

"No, I guess not."

"Well, how do you know your father didn't see Pilaria, too? Maybe she was showing herself to anyone who came along."

"Oh no! She wouldn't!"

"Is your father still home this morning?"

"I don't know. I don't want to see him, anyway."

"That may be," Georgina said sternly, "but I think we had better do a little investigation to find out what he knows. Pilaria might not be safe otherwise. We should start right away, at breakfast!"

"Oh, do we have to?" Angela wailed. "I'm so embarrassed after last night."

"We have to," Georgina decreed. And so, with great nervousness, the group finished dressing and descended to the kitchen.

In line with all the newness and plushness of the Harrall home, the Harralls' kitchen was also a beautiful place. It had recently been done over so that the morning sun could flood through the windows. The stove was on a built-in island at the room's center. Three ovens clung to the walls, and the counters were filled with every sort of modern appliance.

The kitchen table was large and comfortable to sit down at, and normally the friends looked forward to having meals there. Not this morning, however, for settled like a large brown toad in the middle of all the brightness and warmth was the fearful shape of Angela's father. The girls caught sight of him as soon as they entered the room, and each of them jumped a little. He was sitting and reading a newspaper at the table.

"Good morning!" Angela's mother sang out when she saw them. She had been leaning, arms crossed, against a kitchen counter, and it seemed that a serious conversation had been under way because her face looked strained, even when she smiled. "I didn't expect you girls up so early. What a night you had!" She threw her arms around Angela's plump shoulders and gave her a hug.

This was a very nice thing to do, as it started things off in a cheerful, nonaccusing way. All three girls smiled, too. Angela's father glanced at them over the top of his newspaper. He was wearing his little reading glasses again.

Behind the lenses, his eyes looked small and unfriendly.

"Good morning," he said stiffly. "I hope you all are . . . I mean to say, I hope you all slept well?"

Before anyone could answer, he set his coffee cup down with a terrible crash and drew the newspaper up until it covered his face again.

"I'll be gone in a minute," his voice continued behind the paper. "I just want to finish this article."

"Oh, don't hurry," Angela's mother said to him. "There's plenty of room for everyone. The girls would love to keep you company. Wouldn't you, girls?"

"Um . . . I guess so."

"Well . . . okay."

Mr. Harrall lowered his paper and gazed at them with eyes that seemed softer than usual. A strange look came over his face, as if he were trying to smile. But a second later, the newspaper went up again.

The friends spent the next several minutes pouring cereal into bowls, cutting wedges of coffee cake, and trying not to drop their napkins on the floor. Every once in a while, they caught Mr. Harrall peering at them from around a corner of his newspaper. Otherwise he remained invisible. It took all of Georgina's courage to steel herself and speak up.

"Mr. Harrall? Is it all right if we ask you something?"

"What?" His elbow jerked and nearly sent his coffee cup to the floor.

"About last night," Georgina went on. "You see, the reason we were all downstairs is that we thought we heard something. We were investigating. We wondered if you saw anything unusual while you were there."

"Unusual?" Mr. Harrall dropped his newspaper and stared at them.

"You know, any strange noises, or . . . lights?" Georgina tried to look casual as she said this.

"Oh, well . . . " Mr. Harrall's eyes flew over to Angela. "No, I . . . I mean I didn't see anything but . . ." He seemed to be having a struggle with his words. His face had turned a dull red. "But I would like to apologize, Angela, for pouncing on you that way. I . . . I . . . don't know what came over me. I didn't mean to get so angry. I've been nervous lately. I've been worried about something else, and you surprised me."

"Oh, that's all right," Angela said, rather mildly considering all that had happened. "We didn't know it had gotten so late."

Her father looked relieved. His eyes brightened. Then, while the friends clutched their cereal spoons because he stuttered and mumbled and had such a hard time asking, he invited Angela to go to a movie with him that afternoon.

"Just the two of us," he said. "Would you like that? You can pick the movie."

After a pause, Angela shook her head.

"I'm sorry but I can't," she said, keeping her eyes on her plate. "I've already made plans. We are supposed to go to Georgina's house and do some things."

"Oh, I see." Mr. Harrall's face sagged. "Maybe another time, then?"

"Maybe," Angela said coldly.

Her father got up from the table and went in the direction of the coat closet.

"Will you be back for lunch?" Angela's mother called after him. "It's Saturday, you know. Martin called. He's coming home early. I was thinking of making something good, like roast beef sandwiches.

"No," came the answer. "I have to be in the office all day. Things have mounted up. I won't be back until late."

A minute later, a door shut, and Mr. Harrall was gone.

"You know," Georgina said to Angela later,

out of Mrs. Harrall's hearing, "your dad was trying to be nice to you. Why didn't you want to go to the movies with him?"

"I just didn't."

"He looked really sad when you turned him down."

"I don't care."

"What do you think? Did he see Pilaria?" Georgina went on. "He was right there. He walked right into the room."

"Are you crazy? Of course he didn't see her," Angela replied in disgust. "Pilaria would never show herself to somebody like my father."

Chapter Eight

(Delivered to the mantelpiece late Sunday night)

Dear Pilaria,

I loved your letter. It's all right if you can't grant wishes anymore. I don't want things like that, anyway. My parents are always buying me presents—clothes and games and stuff. They even gave me a TV of my own. I have it in my room, but I don't like to watch it. I feel sort of lonely sitting there all by myself.

Now I have seen you two times. Maybe

you didn't know, but the first time was a few days ago when you went down the hall to the living room late at night. Well, you probably did know. Thank you for letting me see you. I feel as if you really trust me and like me. I hope my dad didn't upset you last night when he came in the room. He doesn't know anything about you, so you don't have to worry. I would never tell him or show him your letters.

I am sorry to hear that your kingdom is in hard times. Georgina says it's that way for everybody these days. I feel sad a lot, too, and I know what you mean about stiff faces. In my house, people don't say what is on their minds, either.

Respectfully yours,
Angela Harrall
Fourth Earth (I guess)

(Received on the mantelpiece on Friday morning)

Angela:

I, Pilaria, known also as the Gray-Eyed Faerie, send greetings from my invisible world. Your letter amazed me. We are not so different as I'd thought. I was sorry to hear that you, also, are lonely sometimes. When I saw you with your friends the other night, I imagined you to be the happiest of mortals.

I am a full-time worker for the Kingdom of the Faeries. This means constant flying to distant parts of the globe. There is a great deal to be done every day. Did you know that we invisibles (as we call ourselves) help birds stay on course during their migrations? We are responsible for informing fish of their position in the vast oceans. We also keep records of volcanic eruptions and earthquakes, big storms, tidal waves, and other natural disasters. It is hard to find time in between to make friends. I'm afraid I have grown out of practice over the years. Can you give me some advice? You are obviously a person who knows about this subject.

Respectfully yours,
Pilaria
of the Kingdom of the Faeries,
Eighth Tribe, Fourth Earth,
Under the Sun-Star Aravan,
May It Shine on Our Land
Forever and Ever

(Delivered to the mantelpiece Saturday night)

DEAR PILARIA,

You are so beautiful. I can't believe you don't have hundreds of friends! When I saw you on the mantelpiece, I could hardly breathe! Do all invisibles have such shining, golden wings?

To make a good friend, you only have to think what things look like from her side. (Or his side.) Sometimes it isn't easy. Georgina makes me mad when she tries to boss me around, so I don't feel like looking from her side anymore. Why shouldI? She isn't looking from my side, either. Poco is a very nice person. I would always be friends with her if she didn't have to talk to those dumb animals all the time.

Respectfully yours,
ANGELA HARRALL

P.S. I don't mean Juliette.

P.P.S. Can you explain what Eighth Tribe, Fourth Earth means? Where is the Sun-Star Aravan?

(Received on Friday morning)

ANGELA:

I, Pilaria, known also as the Gray-Eyed Faerie, send sincere thanks for your advice on the matter of friends. I had not thought about them in that way before. I will try it.

You asked about Eighth Tribe, Fourth Earth, etc. They describe my time and place in the cosmos. The Kingdom of the Faeries is very ancient. Invisibles were here on earth from earliest times, and have existed through three different ages on this planet. First Earth was a time of bare land and mighty oceans. Second Earth was warm and saw the rise of jungles. During Third Earth the first animals and birds made their appearance. It is only during the present Fourth Earth that you mortals have appeared among us.

There are presently ten tribes of faeries wandering the planet Earth. I am a member of the eighth.

Have I said that Aravan is an ancient name for the sun? We are all (animals, plants, mortals, and invisibles) under the Sun-Star Aravan together. All of us would be lost if our great yellow star should cease its glow.

I am golden to your eye. To others, I may appear in different colors. And shapes.

Respectfully yours,
PILARIA
of the K. of the F.,
E.T., F.E.,
U.T.S.S.A.,
M.I.S.O.O.L.F.&E.

(Delivered to the mantelpiece on Saturday night)

DEAR PILARIA,

My friends Poco and Georgina are very interested in you. They wanted me to ask if you would let them see you. Would next Friday night be all right? My brother will be away on a football trip and my father has to go to South America on business. Please say yes.

Respectfully,
ANGELA HARRALL
Fourth Earth,
U.T.S.S.A.,
M.I.S.O.O.L.F.&E.

(Received Monday morning)

ANGELA:

I, Pilaria, known also as the Gray-Eyed Faerie, am pleased to grant your wish.

On the morning that Angela received this last letter, the three friends went into a state of wild, barely controlled excitement. They walked the halls at school with glowing eyes. They met around corners for mysterious conversations and passed notes to each other during classes.

At lunch, they could be seen forgetting to eat their sandwiches as they spoke in low voices at a table near the wall. But the worst was soccer practice, where they had to be separated three times by Mr. Corelli, the coach, for bunching together and talking on the field.

"Girls!" he howled. "Where is our team spirit? Where is our defense? The goal is wide open to enemy attack! Must we have a summit conference after every play?"

"No, Mr. Corelli."

"Sorry, Mr. Corelli."

"Good grief!" Georgina whispered to Poco, as they sat together briefly on the sidelines bench. "School is getting more impossible every day. They herd us like cattle from class to class, and scramble our brains with formulas and rules, and then they take away the one thing every American—man, woman, and child—has a right to in this country."

"What's that?" Poco asked.

"Freedom of speech!" Georgina hissed, with a furious glance at Mr. Corelli. "It's written in the Constitution, in case you didn't know."

Poco had heard about this vaguely before, but somehow had never applied it to real life.

"That is so interesting!" she said. "A lot of friends of mine have exactly the same trouble. Rabbits, for instance. They've had to keep their voices low for years because no one likes the sound of their high little shrieks. The only time you hear a rabbit really talk is when it's stuck somewhere or about to be killed."

Georgina was opening her mouth to tell Poco that this was, by far, the weirdest remark she had ever made, when Mr. Corelli ordered them both back onto the field. They brushed past Angela coming toward the bench, but no one dared to stop and talk. By now, Mr. Corelli was stamping around like a power-mad military dictator and not allowing anyone even to pass the ball without his permission.

Pilaria's promise to appear before the group was incredible and miraculous but, like many miracles, it was going to require some management to put into action. The friends had no illusions about this. They went to work immediately after school that afternoon.

First, and most difficult, was the problem of persuading Angela's mother to allow another sleepover so soon after the first.

"Especially since we were not exactly perfect guests the last time," Georgina pointed out. The three were walking along the sidewalk toward the Rusk home, where they planned to consult at length.

"Maybe she's forgiven us," Angela said. "She was terribly nice the next morning at breakfast. And she's never mentioned it since."

"Are you sure your father won't be there?" Georgina asked. "I don't think my nerves could stand running into him again."

"Positive. He left this morning for a week. Something happened in his business down in South America. My mother is furious because he waited until the last minute to tell her."

"I guess the best way is for you to ask your mom tonight, then," Georgina went on. "And try to break down her arguments one by one."

"Oh no," said Poco, who had been trailing behind gazing up into trees along the street. "The best way is for all three of us to go and ask her. Then she won't have any arguments."

"Why not?" asked Angela and Georgina, slowing down to walk with her.

"It's a well-known tactic in the bird world," Poco said with a shrug. "Say you're a wild duck, and you want to persuade another wild duck to fly south with you for the winter. If you go to her and say, 'Let's fly south,' she'll probably have all these reasons why she doesn't want to leave right now, or she doesn't like the route you picked, or something. It's duck nature to be grumpy about new ideas. But if a group of ducks decides, 'We are going south for the winter!' then the one duck is a lot more likely to be persuaded. She doesn't want to make a fuss and look bad in front of the others. Besides, the trip begins to sound like more fun."

Angela and Georgina had stopped walking by the time Poco finished. They stared in awe at their friend.

"That is so right!" Georgina exclaimed after a moment.

"It sounds just like my mother, too," Angela said. "She'd hate to disappoint all three of us at once."

"Where do you pick up these things?" asked Georgina, her eyes narrowing into their old suspicious squint. "I know it's not really from birds."

"It most certainly is from birds!" Poco declared.

"Of course it's from birds," Angela said. She gave Georgina a warning look. "Poco should know where she gets her information."

Georgina sighed. "Okay, okay. In that case, what are we doing walking to my house? We should be going to Angela's to talk to her mother."

At this, as if they were a flock of wild ducks themselves, the three friends spun around in a single swoop and began to walk briskly in the opposite direction.

Chapter Nine

Poco's bird tactic worked so well on Mrs. Harrall that, before she knew it, she had agreed to take the group to a movie on Friday night, as well as allow another sleepover. She insisted on only one thing.

"You must all be in bed no later than midnight," she told the friends. "That is reasonable, don't you think? A little too reasonable for your age, in fact, so please don't tell your mothers, Poco and Georgina. They will think me weak-kneed and unable to stand up to children. Then I won't be allowed to hold sleepovers in the future."

Everybody laughed at this. "Don't worry, Mom," Angela said. "No one will tell."

"Mrs. Harrall, you are the best mother," Poco exclaimed. "Would it be all right if Juliette spent the night with us, too? In Angela's room, I mean, instead of under the radiator? She could sleep in my bed. I wouldn't mind at all. She doesn't get invited to very many sleepovers, you know."

"Oh, certainly," said Mrs. Harrall, giving Poco a curious glance. "How kind of you to think of her."

So the night was arranged, and the friends settled down to wait out the week. By Friday, they were twitching with impatience. In the afternoon, Georgina and Poco walked home with Angela, as they had on the other Friday. There was no need to investigate the house this time, however. Angela had received no new letters all week. She had not sent any letters to Pilaria either, wanting not to bother her at such a delicate moment.

The minute they arrived at the Harralls' house, Poco went to speak to Juliette. But the cat was dull and unresponsive, and kept falling asleep in the middle of questions. It was as if her cat spirit had flown off somewhere, leaving the big, lumpy body sprawled behind on the floor.

"Juliette. For goodness' sakes! What is wrong with you?" Poco cried.

Georgina pursed her lips. "I expect I know," she said. "I expect she's sick of acting like a person and has decided to act like a plain old fat cat for a while. Everybody needs a vacation, you know."

Poco scowled.

At five o'clock the group ate an early supper. At six, they went with Mrs. Harrall to the movie theater, where they sat and wiggled through the film like a group of three-year-olds.

"This movie seems so stupid and fake," Georgina whispered to Angela when the first half hour had gone by. "I can hardly wait to get back to your house. Do you think Pilaria will look different to us than she does to you? Remember in her letter when she said—"

A loud shushing came from the person sitting behind them. Georgina shut her mouth and slouched angrily in her seat.

"Did you bring your mom's camera again?" Poco whispered to Georgina a little later.

"Yes! And this time I won't forget about it. I'm going to get a picture of Pilaria no matter what."

By nine o'clock, they were home again, wandering about the house with restless eyes. Angela's mother looked tired. She had hardly spoken all evening, which was unusual for her.

"If you girls don't mind, I think I'll go to bed," she said apologetically. "I started working longer hours at the bank this week. I'm all worn out. I know you will take care of yourselves."

"We will. Good-night."

"Sweet dreams."

"Good-night."

"Sleep well. Nighty-night."

"Night."

"Good grief!" Georgina's jaw clenched in exasperation.

"Everything is so boringly ordinary!" she exploded, when Mrs. Harrall had finally disappeared into her room. They were all sitting on Angela's bed. "First dinner, then a movie, then those horrible nighty-nights. I can't stand it anymore! This is beginning to seem like every other sleepover that ever was in the world. When is something interesting going to happen?"

There was the briefest of silences after this outburst, just long enough to hear a few notes from Mrs. Harrall's classical music station float down the hall. Then, incredibly, something did happen.

Very slowly, the door of Angela's room began to move. Inch by inch it swung into the room until it was about halfway open. With a ghostly squeak, it came to a halt. A large gray shadow shot across the threshold and disappeared under the bed.

"What was that!" whispered Angela.

Georgina's eyes grew round with fright.

Poco rose to her knees and bent over to lift up Angela's bedspread.

"It's Juliette!" she cried, as the cat sauntered back into view. "Look, she's come awake!"

There was no doubt that Juliette wished to tell them something. She padded over to the middle of the rug, looked up with wide, anxious eyes, and mewed. When no one moved, she mewed again, long and plaintively. She sat down and began to lick a paw.

"What's she saying?" Georgina asked Poco, without taking her eyes off the cat.

"There's someone downstairs," Poco answered softly. "Juliette is telling us that someone has come."

Angela sucked in her breath. "Who?"

"She isn't saying," Poco replied. "But it might be—"

"Pilaria!"

"Not already," objected Georgina. "It's too early."

Angela climbed off the bed. Juliette was on her feet again and had started to walk toward the door. When she reached it, she paused and looked back at them.

"She wants us to follow her," Angela said. "I can understand that without even speaking Siamese."

Poco and Georgina slid off the bed and the three girls went quietly across the room. They paused in the doorway. Mrs. Harrall had turned out the hall lights. The whole house was in blackness.

"Should I get my flashlight?" Angela asked.

Georgina shook her head. "Not enough time," she whispered, thinking suddenly of the camera. No wonder magic beings were so rarely photographed. There was never enough time to catch them in the act. "Look! There goes Juliette."

A flash of gray streaked away down the hall and disappeared in the dark. The girls crept out and followed. When they reached the stairs, they looked down. A pale glow was coming from the living room. It cast a dim rectangle of light into the hall—just as before. Only now—what was that? The friends' eyes opened wide. The dark figure of a cat stood poised upon the threshold.

"How did Juliette get downstairs so fast?" Georgina whispered. "It's not natural."

Poco didn't answer. Angela was already starting to descend. They moved together down the stairs, a close, nervous band of white faces and cold hands. The air in the hall seemed thick, unbreathable.

"Angela! Wait! Juliette has disappeared," Georgina whispered.

"She went in the living room."

"No, there she is again!"

"Keep going. Hurry up!"

The old cat seemed worried about losing them. She stalked in and out across the doorway, gazing sometimes into the room, sometimes at the approaching group. They reached the bottom step and moved out into the hall. The dim light in the living room flickered suddenly, as if it were beckoning. They crept to the doorway and peeped in.

There, just as Angela had described it before, their first impression was that a small, powerful fire had sprung up in the middle of the mantelpiece—three feet above where a fire should be burning. Poco covered her mouth with both hands. Georgina stared.

"Pilaria?" Angela asked, a quaver in her voice. "Is that you?"

The light danced and waved.

"I've brought my friends. Here they are."

Poco stepped forward, followed by Georgina.

"Can we come closer?" Angela asked respectfully. The group tiptoed across and stopped about ten feet away.

"She is spinning around," Georgina whispered.

"I see a lot of lighted candles," Poco said.

"What are those gold things?" Georgina inquired. "Hey, wait a minute!"

Angela shifted her weight uneasily.

"Wait a minute!" Georgina said again. "This isn't Pilaria. It's a candle carousel. We used to have one at our house, only with gold angels flying around instead of"—she stepped up closer—"instead of these little whatever-they-ares."

"What are they?" Angela asked weakly.

"I don't know. Fireflies, maybe. They look like little bugs with wings. They're made of brass or something. The heat from the candles makes them spin around. That's why it's called a candle carousel."

Angela's face had taken on a collapsed look.

"Is this the thing you saw the other night?" Georgina demanded in loud, suspicious tones. "Because if it is, it's not magic. You see them all over the place in the stores around the holidays."

Now Angela appeared on the verge of tears. Poco stepped forward.

"What's that?" she asked, pointing.

"Where?" Georgina turned to see.

"On the mantelpiece next to the candles."

Angela saw it, too. She reached out eagerly to grasp the familiar-looking scroll of paper. It was tied with a thin gold thread. As the others watched, she slipped off the thread and began to unroll the paper. And though everyone had forgotten to expect it because the moment was so tense, a tremendous waterfall of gold dust poured suddenly between her fingers and tumbled and twinkled its way toward the floor.

"That was the most gold dust ever!" Georgina exclaimed. Angela hardly noticed. She wrenched the letter open and started to read it.

"Pilaria has left us a message," she announced in a relieved voice. "She has invited us to a fairy banquet. Right now. In the kitchen."

"Right now! Are you sure?" Georgina came around to read for herself.

"To Angela Harrall and Her Two Friends:

Pilaria, known also as the Gray-Eyed Faerie, humbly requests the pleasure of your company at a Faerie Banquet in the Kitchen, in honor of Our Friendship. Please come at your convenience.

Respectfully yours,
Pilaria,
Eighth Tribe,
Fourth Earth, etc., etc."

Georgina looked up from the letter. Poco's hands had flown to her face again. "In the kitchen!" she cried. "That's Juliette's place. And where is she, anyway?"

They looked around the room. Juliette had disappeared.

Angela allowed the letter to roll up with a snap. Keeping it in her hand, she began to walk out of the living room. Poco and Georgina followed silently. Down the hall they marched, toward the back of the house. Though it was dark in this section, they had not gone far when a faint light began to appear ahead.

Someone was in the kitchen, there could be no doubt. As they went closer, little rustling sounds and noises of movement came to their ears. And a mysterious smell, half sweet and half musty, met their nostrils. Angela clutched Poco, who reached for Georgina's hand. Then, with pounding hearts, the friends rounded the corner together, determined to see the real Gray-Eyed Faerie at last.

Chapter Ten

It would not be enough to say that the Harralls' kitchen was a changed place. When something is changed, a new thing comes and takes over the old. But the old part is still there, still visible in places. It lies quietly under the surface with its familiar shapes and ways, reminding you of just what was changed into what.

To Angela and Poco and Georgina, the kitchen that appeared before their eyes that night had not changed. It had vanished. Nothing was familiar in the shapes that met their gaze.

Nothing lay beneath the surface. Everything had been swept away. And in its place . . .

Angela drew in a deep breath and let it out slowly. "Oh, Pilaria," she murmured. "How beautiful!"

The room was bathed in golden light. As if a golden moon had dropped down from the sky, the air itself seemed to twinkle and shine. Candles were everywhere, lighting every corner and ledge. And hanging from the ceiling were long veils of golden cloth, glistening chains of glass, and bright silver flowers the size of umbrellas. The kitchen walls seemed to have dissolved completely, and there, off in the distance, a sprinkle of stars lit some magical outer space.

But that wasn't all. That was only the background to the wonderful vision that floated front and center before the friends' eyes. It was a table set for three, covered with shells and sparkling confetti and a wild tangle of flowers. In the place of plates were giant golden leaves. And where the napkins usually went, they saw small pairs of white gloves.

The cups were long-stemmed goblets, half-filled with a golden liquid. Other leaf plates lay about the table. Upon them could be seen strange little cakes and layered sandwiches, slices of fruit, and sugared nuts. A shiny green leaf plate held a mound of the tiniest strawberries Angela had ever seen. And on another leaf—what were those pale, circular slivers? Shavings of white chocolate? Angela leaned forward and squinted into the candles' glare.

It was then she saw something move, beyond the table. Back in the corner, a figure was standing in shadow. When the figure saw that it was noticed, it attempted to move farther into the dark. And indeed it might really have slipped away—it was already heading shyly for the back door—if Angela had not gone quickly toward it and stood in its path.

"Pilaria?" she asked, looking up at the form. Poco and Georgina stared wide-eyed from across the room.

"Yes. Oh dear, I'm afraid you've really caught me this time," the form replied. "You came much earlier than I expected. But . . . don't let me interfere. This is your banquet to enjoy. Go right ahead and sit down. All of you are welcome!"

A rather long and frightening pause followed this amazing statement. Angela, who continued looking up, seemed to sway and then to sag a bit on her feet. For a moment, her chin trembled, as if she were about to cry. But then, with sudden resolve, she drew herself up straight.

"But . . . aren't you going to sit down, too?" she asked the form in a clear voice. "There's plenty of room for everyone."

"Well, I . . ." The form stammered and hesitated. "Of course, if you wouldn't mind."

"Not at all. We'd like it," Angela answered, drawing the form toward the table. Only then did Poco and Georgina see who it was.

"Mr. Harrall!" Georgina gasped. Poco looked stunned.

But Angela shook her head. "Not tonight," she said. "Tonight I would like to introduce you to"—she turned toward him respectfully—"Pilaria, of the Kingdom of the Faeries, Eighth Tribe, Fourth Earth, Under the Sun-Star Aravan, May It Shine on Our Land Forever and Ever."

Pilaria was seen to glance around nervously at this. But he managed a small smile.

"I am more pleased to meet you than you will ever know," he told the group, and bent over and gave them the humblest and nicest bow.

Later, the friends would understand how everything had been accomplished. They would see, for instance, that the banquet's golden veils were really camp mosquito netting turned golden by the candles' light; that the glass chains were made of plastic; that the leaf plates had been traced and cut from gold paper; that even the faraway planets and stars had a more local origin—they came from Angela's old Night Sky toy, which cast constellations in shining dots upon the ceiling and across the walls.

Later the magic would lift like mist along a river, and the Harrall kitchen would return to view, and the table would stand square on the floor again. Later . . . but not now.

Now, despite Pilaria's shocking revelation, somehow the magic was still at work. It swirled about the banquet table in the most exciting way. First Poco, and then even Georgina, allowed herself to come forward and be charmed. They sat down under the veils and admired the little cakes and slices of fruit. They examined the shells and picked up some white stones with holes in them that lay near the leaf plates. They tasted the strawberries and sipped the golden liquid (it was honeyed lemonade). And put on their white gloves.

What these were for no one could imagine—until Pilaria, seeing their confusion, spoke up in an apologetic voice. He had not uttered a word while the group had examined the table, but had hovered anxiously behind their chairs.

"I'm sorry, I should have explained," he said, sitting beside Angela at last. "They are fairy handshakes."

"Fairy what?"

"You know, napkins."

Apparently, the table manners of invisibles were far more advanced than those of mortals, who continued to use ridiculous little cloth or paper squares at meals, which were always falling off their laps and causing conversation to be interrupted.

"Handshakes are better than napkins by every measure," Pilaria explained. "You can really wipe your mouth with the back of your hand, not just dab when no one's looking. And there are two, one for each side, so there's always help close by."

He looked uneasy as he said this, and glanced at the friends to see how they would take it. When they laughed, he was relieved and seemed genuinely pleased. He was, in many ways, an alien creature, and so obviously unused to associating with human beings—or with human girls, anyway—that the friends began to feel sorry for him. Though he resembled, in appearance, the person they had known before as Angela's father, all other signs of that disturbing figure had disappeared.

"What are these strange white stones with holes in them?" Poco asked, to keep the conversation going.

"Oh, those are charms to ward off fairy powers," Pilaria replied. "It is easy for mortals to fall under an invisible's spell, and some fairies are not so nice as others."

"And this horseshoe?"

"The same. A shield against spells. You could also turn your sweaters inside out. It keeps mischievous invisibles under control. Not me," he added hastily, gazing at them in alarm. "I am not playing or pretending."

The friends nodded. They felt his seriousness. It was why the banquet's magic was continuing to work.

"The shells, by the way, are fairy coaches," Pilaria went on. "They are the way most invisibles travel about in the world, though we humans never see them. Fairies are careful to turn their shells invisible, too."

Georgina sat up suddenly. "Wait a minute! Where did you learn all this?" she demanded. "I know it's not from fairies. You read some book, right?"

Angela and Poco were horrified by this

rudeness, and looked to see if Pilaria would be angry. But he seemed not to mind.

"It *is* from fairies, actually," he said. "You know, I used to write to some myself."

"You did!" Angela was amazed.

"When I was young. I took quite an interest in invisibles of all sorts in those days. And I believed, really and truly, in the answers I received. Most of them were from my mother, I found out later. But there were a few . . ." Pilaria paused and looked thoughtfully at the group. He reached out and picked up a white pebble and turned it about so that it gleamed in the candlelight.

"There were a few letters that could not be accounted for," he went on, slowly. "That's how magic is, I suppose. It really happens only once in a while, and afterward—"

"You forget you saw it," Angela finished in excitement. "Or people tell you you're crazy, so you don't believe what you saw anymore."

Pilaria nodded. He put the white stone back on the table.

"That's right," he said. "That's exactly what happened to me. Over the years, I completely forgot about those letters, and about invisibles, and I didn't believe in magic anymore. I'd even nearly forgotten about the candle carousel."

Angela's head jerked up. "What about it?" she asked. "When we saw it on the mantelpiece, we thought it was a magic being." Poco and Georgina nodded.

"I used to think so, too," Pilaria replied. "For many years, when I was small, that carousel appeared in my family's house. At certain holiday times during the year, it was lit at night. I used to stare at it and imagine the little spinning figures were invisibles who'd crossed over into our world. That's why, when Angela wrote a letter to her fairy godmother . . ." He paused uncertainly.

"You remembered. And answered!" Poco declared.

"Yes." He looked at Angela in such a way that the candlelight caught his eyes and everyone saw their color.

"The Gray-Eyed Faerie," Georgina murmured. "You really do have gray eyes!"

Pilaria glanced down. "I wasn't trying to play a trick," he said. "I wanted to be friends. Martin and I have stayed on good terms. But Angela . . ." He turned toward her shyly. "You always seemed so far away from me. I didn't know how to talk to you. I decided to give you the candle carousel as a special present—from Pilaria, of course—to bring you closer."

"Then what Angela saw the first night on the

mantelpiece really was the candle carousel?" Georgina asked.

"Yes. I lit it and set it going. But then you all appeared and surprised me. I was embarrassed and acted badly, I'm afraid. It had been so long since I'd believed in other worlds. I guess I hadn't quite gotten the feel of it yet. Can you forgive me, do you think?"

Angela nodded gravely. "Your letters were beautiful," she said. "How did you write them?"

Pilaria shrugged modestly. "It's a little talent I have," he said. "I used to be quite good at calligraphy. The purple ink and paper are old equipment from the past. They were up in the attic—another thing I'd forgotten all about!" He smiled. "First and Second Earths," he added. "Those were the days!"

"So, a lot of what you wrote in the letters was true," Georgina declared.

"Yes. Quite true. Though I don't go around recording major disasters or advising birds and fish of their locations. My real job is not so important as that."

"But where did you keep the paper and ink?" Georgina asked. "We looked and looked for it."

"Oh, in my briefcase," Pilaria said. "It traveled with me wherever I went."

There was a sudden scuffle under the table. Poco leaned down and came up with . . .

"Juliette! You silly thing. What are you doing slithering around under there!"

Everyone laughed. The old Siamese looked hurt.

"It was Juliette who came and told us you were here," Angela said to Pilaria. "We'd started to think she was an invisible in disguise. She acted so suspicious all the time."

"Siamese cats always act suspicious. It's part of their nature," Poco said. "Nothing compared to bats, though. They are the most suspicious-acting creatures of all. You can never tell what a bat has up his sleeve."

"Up his sleeve! Oh, Poco, ugh!" Georgina shivered all over at the thought of bats in sleeves.

"Now that is truly interesting," Pilaria said, leaning forward. "I used to know a bat when I was younger. He lived in my bedroom, under the eaves, and liked to come out and fly around at night. I provided him with food—insects and such—and left the window open so he could go off. He always came back, but . . . Now that you mention it, Poco, he was mysterious. I suspected him of many things, including stalking people on the road after dark. I sometimes heard their frightened screams."

"How horrible!" Angela exclaimed. "Do you think he was a vampire?"

Georgina went absolutely white when she heard this, and stood up and quickly turned her sweater inside out. Afterward, a lively discussion erupted about suspicious things of all sorts. The layered sandwiches and cakes were gobbled up, and almost everything else as well. In fact, the banquet was going so wonderfully, and there were so many fascinating things to talk about, that not until quite a while later was there a lull in the conversation. In the sudden quiet, Angela looked over at Pilaria. She had a question for him that she had been saving.

"What about the dust?" she asked.

"The dust?" Pilaria reached for the last sugared nut. "What do you mean?"

"You know, the gold dust. It always flew out of the letters whenever we opened them. What was it made of, and how did it work?"

The silence in the room became complete. All three friends gazed at Pilaria, who stared back at them with a bewildered expression.

"I'm afraid," he said at last, "that I know nothing about any dust."

"Yes you do!" Angela protested. "You remember, the gold dust. We want to know how it was done. It flew out—poof!—whenever we opened a letter. But no matter how hard we looked, we could never find anything inside."

Pilaria listened carefully while Angela finished this explanation. Then, to the horror of the friends, he shook his head a second time.

"I'm sorry," he said. "I don't know anything about it. And that is the honest-to-goodness truth."

Chapter Eleven

There was no help for it. Angela's father simply refused to admit to the gold dust. The layered sandwiches, yes, he had made them. The golden leaf plates, yes, he had cut them out himself.

He had transformed the kitchen and set the enchanted table and written the beautiful letters and lit the candle carousel. He had done so many things that Angela would never have believed he could do, in fact, that to her it seemed like a kind of magic. It was as if her father really had been invisible before, and had decided, suddenly, to come out and be seen.

That night during the banquet, Angela stared and stared at him. Before her eyes, he turned younger, and happier, and gentler, and kinder, and more open and interesting in every way. Though she could not completely trust these changes yet, she began to want to find out more about him. He began to seem like the sort of person another person might be friends with.

Only about the gold dust did he refuse to explain. He refused many more times that night—until the friends' eyes began to droop, and they agreed, at last, to go to bed. (How they hated to end the banquet, though. It was as real as any fairy's ever was, they said.)

He refused the next morning when, changed back into Mr. Harrall in his business suit, he greeted them all at breakfast.

"Well! What a night you girls had!" he boomed out when they arrived, rather late, in the kitchen. He winked at Angela and handed Georgina a glass of orange juice.

Mrs. Harrall, who was cooking pancakes at the stove, looked around in surprise.

"Were the girls still up when you got home?" she asked him. "I forgot to tell them you were coming back from South America earlier than expected. Thank you," she added, a bit severely, "for calling and letting me know your plans ahead of time. For once."

Angela and Georgina saw Mr. Harrall's jaw tighten. He was about to say something back when Poco sat down next to him with a plate of pancakes. Catching his eye, she drew a pair of white gloves from her pocket and put them on.

"I've heard that South America is where a lot of vampire bats hang out," Poco said, picking up her fork. "Did you happen to see any when you were there?"

"Not a single one. I'm sorry," Mr. Harrall answered, with a pleased expression. He started to butter his pancakes. "But that doesn't mean anything. Vampires never show themselves to businessmen. They have no interest in such people."

"I suppose it's because businessmen are too tough." Georgina said, sitting down on Mr. Harrall's other side and taking out her gloves. "The vampires have trouble getting through to their blood."

"That is very likely," Mr. Harrall said, smiling grimly.

Angela brought her plate to the table and drew up a chair across from her father. She took out a pair of white gloves and put them on, too.

"There are some people who say that if a businessman has a certain kind of dust," she began, "a certain, special kind of gold dust, it softens him up a lot. Then he has to watch out for vampires like everybody else."

Mr. Harrall cleared his throat. "That may be," he replied, "but I did not have such dust on my trip. And I don't have any now. But I do have some shells, and these stones with holes in them, that you might be interested in." He reached into his suit pocket and brought out several handfuls of things, which he placed in the middle of the table. "You forgot them and, who knows, they might come in handy."

"Oh yes!" The friends leaned over the pile to choose the ones they knew to be theirs.

Mrs. Harrall had turned all the way around from the stove by this time. She was staring at the gloves, and at the shells and stones, and at everyone in confusion.

"What is going on this morning!" she exclaimed. "I think I've missed something."

She turned off the stove and sat down at the table, and demanded to know what had happened last night. ("Because I can see something did!" she said.) So the three friends chimed in and told her about Pilaria, and the letters, and the extraordinary fairy banquet. They explained what fairy handshakes were, and how to protect yourself against spells. Angela's mother was astonished. She looked at Angela's father with disbelieving eyes.

"You did all this?"

"I'm afraid so."

"Magic letters on the mantelpiece? It sounds so unlike you."

"I suppose it does."

"And a banquet? You must have cleaned up after yourself. There wasn't a fork or a plate out of place when I came down this morning."

"There weren't any forks or plates used," Angela put in quickly. "Everything was made or specially invented."

"Well, I am completely amazed," Mrs. Harrall said to Mr. Harrall, a frown gathering on her brow. "I never would have thought you had time for such things. You certainly never had time before."

"So it seemed," Mr. Harrall replied, "but I found some." He glanced unhappily across the table at his wife. "I found some time and magic I didn't know I had."

Then, though it was Saturday, he pushed back his chair and went off to work. The friends were relieved to see him go. His face had turned stiff and angry again. Only after the back door had slammed behind him, and Angela's mother had stood abruptly and gone upstairs, did the three girls remember the really important thing. There was still—still!—no explanation for the gold dust.

A whole week passed before the group could meet alone again. The sleepover had been magical and wonderful, but now real life rose up like a mighty river and swept everyone and everything into its stream.

School took a great deal of concentration. And after school, Poco had math tutoring, or Georgina had to visit the dentist, or Angela was picked up by her mother to go shopping. Though these distractions did not stop the friends from thinking, they had no chance for conversation with each other.

So it was with a sense of time passing and mysteries waiting that they gathered in Georgina's backyard on a chilly Saturday morning the next weekend. There were a hundred things to talk about. If only the wind were not so cold!

"I am beginning to think," said Georgina with a shiver, "that, even though it's impossible, Angela's father must be telling the truth. He really doesn't seem to know anything about the gold dust."

Angela raised her head. They were sitting in a sort of huddle on the grass. "I forgot to tell you. It's stopped," she said. "No dust comes out of the letters anymore. I've opened each one of them, many times. The writing is the same, but there's nothing inside." Her face appeared thinner and whiter than usual. She leaned back and gazed bleakly at the sky.

"Are you all right?" Poco asked her. "You look a little down."

Georgina scowled. "Let's stick to the issues, okay?" she snapped. "Our investigation is almost finished. There's just this last maddening piece that won't fit into the puzzle. I'm sure there's an answer. What else has been going on over at your house lately?" she asked Angela. "Any more lights or strange things happening?"

"No." Angela took her hands out of her pockets and rolled over heavily onto her stomach. "My father moved out. He's getting an apartment. Not far from here. Pretty close, really. I get to go and visit him next weekend."

"Oh, Angela. That's terrible!" Poco put her arm around Angela's shoulders. Georgina looked shaken.

"Did your parents have a fight?" she asked. "They didn't seem that bad when we were there."

Angela shrugged. "Not really."

"Well, what happened?"

"I don't know."

"Well, something must have happened," Georgina said. "Otherwise they would still be together."

"It's not explainable."

"What do you mean, it's not explainable? Everything's explainable!"

"George!" cried Poco.

Angela looked at Georgina levelly. "My mom's been a lot happier since my dad left," she said. "She doesn't even mind that my brother might go to live with him for a while. She says we're all reasonable people and can work it out."

"Do you think you will?" Georgina asked.

"I don't know." Angela pulled some blades of grass out of the lawn. "My dad is being really nice. We've been getting friendlier and friendlier. I might even go to South America with him on a business trip sometime. He says he wants to show me a real vampire bat."

The friends laughed.

"Well, everybody knows that your mom is the best mother," Poco said. "At least you don't have to be mad at anyone."

Angela reached out and yanked up a whole tuft of grass. "But I am," she said in a low, trembling voice. "At both of them. Why did they have to wreck our family?" Tears dropped suddenly down her cheeks.

Poco hugged her again. "You've still got us," she whispered. "We'll always be your friends."

Georgina knotted her fist. "It's like that stupid gold dust," she said angrily to Angela. "It makes me so mad I feel like crying, too. How could anything like that happen? We all saw it. We know it was real. But it's unexplainable. There's no way the dust could have got in the letters."

"Oh, that's easy." Angela sniffed. "That was magic."

Poco nodded. "I think the gold dust was one of those incredible pieces of real magic that rise up out of the unknown," she said. "And now we're going to start wondering what we really saw. Or people will say we're crazy. Or we'll grow up like Angela's dad and forget everything."

"Not me," Georgina said. "I'll never forget."

"Me, either," said Poco and Angela together.

They all looked fiercely at one another.

"Maybe the unknown is not so unusual," Georgina continued after a moment. "Maybe there are a lot of unexplainable things that happen every day, only people don't usually notice. You know, because everyone is working nonstop and going through hard times. I was thinking that we might want to start a special operation."

"What kind of operation?" Poco asked.

"Investigating," Georgina said. "We could be secret investigators of unexplainable things."

"Investigators of the unknown!" Angela said, sitting up.

"Right! I would like to find out more about invisibles, for instance," Georgina declared. "If the gold dust was real, that means there must have been other powers at work in your house that we didn't see. Maybe your dad was getting some help."

"Maybe," Angela said.

"And we never did get the full story on Juliette. She could be at the bottom of everything."

"That's true," Poco said. "Juliette has a most maddening way of talking in circles. It's hard to tell where she begins from where she ends. Of course, that is nothing compared to spiders, who can get you tied up in complete knots. Or circus ponies . . ."

Angela shot a warning glance at Georgina, who immediately raised both hands to her mouth and called through them.

"All Investigators of the Unknown will please report to the Rusks' kitchen immediately for popcorn and hot chocolate," she announced in a long bellow, "before we freeze out here and turn into invisibles ourselves!"

"Okay! Let's go!" cried Angela, jumping up.

"Or ringworms," Poco was continuing on. "Not that I have ever talked to a ringworm, but I've read that they—"

She was grabbed by two pairs of hands, hoisted to her feet, and hauled away across the lawn.